P9-EDS-052

SADIQ and the Ramadan Gift

BY SIMAN NUURALI

ART BY ANJAN SARKAR

PICTURE WINDOW BOOKS
a capstone imprint

Sadiq is published by Picture Window Books, an imprint of Capstone.
1710 Roe Crest Drive
North Mankato, Minnesota 56003
www.capstonepub.com

Library of Congress Cataloging-in-Publication Data is available on the Library of Congress website.

ISBN: 978-1-5158-7102-6 (hardcover)
ISBN: 978-1-5158-7134-7 (eBook pdf)
ISBN: 978-1-5158-7288-7 (paperback)

Summary: It's Ramadan! In the spirit of the season, Sadiq and his friends want to give back to their community. The friends band together to raise money for schoolchildren in Somalia. They decide to put on a community iftar as a fundraiser, but not everyone agrees where their efforts should be spent. Can they find a way to work together?

Design Element: Shutterstock/Irtsya

Designer: Brann Garvey

Printed in the United States of America.
3342

TABLE OF CONTENTS

HI, I'M SADIQ! MY FAMILY AND I LIVE IN MINNESOTA, BUT MY PARENTS ARE FROM SOMALIA. SOMETIMES WE SPEAK SOMALI AT HOME.
I'D LIKE YOU TO MEET MY FAMILY AND LEARN SOME INTERESTING FACTS AND TERMS FROM OUR CULTURE.
Baba
Hooyo
Nuurali
Aliya
Rania
Amina

FACTS ABOUT SOMALIA

- Somali people come from many different clans.
- Many Somalis are nomadic. That means they travel from place to place. They search for water, food, and land for their animals.
- Somalia is mostly desert. It doesn't rain often there.
- The camel is an important animal to Somali people. Camels can survive a long time without food or water.
- Around ninety-nine percent of all Somalis are Muslim.

SOMALI TERMS

baba (BAH-baah)—a common word for father

habo (HAA-bo)—aunt; or a term for a Somali woman

hooyo (HOY-yoh)—mother

iftar (IF-tahr)—a meal taken by Muslims at sundown to break the fast during Ramadan

imam (ih-MAHM)—the Muslim leader of a mosque

ma'alin (MAH-leen)—teacher

masjid (MAHS-jid)—mosque; a place where Muslims worship

sadaqah (sah-DAH-kah)—charity

salaam (sa-LAHM)—a short form of greeting, used by many Muslims. It also means "peace."

CHAPTER 1

RAMADAN IS HERE!

It was a warm Sunday afternoon in April. Sadiq, Zaza, and Manny were about to leave Dugsi.

"Does everyone remember when Ramadan starts this week?" asked their teacher, Mr. Kassim.

"Not until the new moon," said Sadiq. "Baba says we have to wait to see it in the sky. He says it is just a sliver when we first see it."

"Yes, Sadiq. That is correct," replied Mr. Kassim, smiling. "Why do we wait until the moon comes out?"

"Because the Islamic calendar follows the moon," said Manny.

"My baba calls it a lunar calendar," Zaza said.

"You're all correct, boys," said Mr. Kassim. "I also want to talk about ***sadaqah***."

"What does that mean, ***Ma'alin***?" asked Manny.

"The meaning of sadaqah is charity. We try to help people in need," said Mr. Kassim. "This year our ***masjid*** will raise money for a Dugsi. The kids at Al-Iqra school in Somalia need one."

"Where do they study now?" asked Zaza.

"They have a classroom. It's just very old and needs repairs," replied Mr. Kassim. "It would be nice to help raise money. The money would help them fix it."

"How can we do that?" asked Manny.

"You know, sometimes people host **iftars** to raise money. Iftars are meals where Muslims break their fast," said Mr. Kassim.

"My hooyo hosted an iftar last year," said Sadiq. "All our neighbors came and broke the fast with us at sundown. It was fun!"

"Wonderful, Sadiq!" said Mr. Kassim. "Another idea to help Al-Iqra might be hosting a bake sale to raise money. Or you could run a school-supply drive for the students."

"What if we don't raise enough money?" asked Zaza.

"Even small donations will help," Mr. Kassim said. "I hope you all can get involved in some way with this effort."

Zaza, Manny, and I could host an iftar, Sadiq thought. *I bet it would raise a lot of money.*

"Charity and giving is an important part of Ramadan. So is fasting. Can anyone tell me why people fast during Ramadan?" asked Mr. Kassim.

Sadiq raised his hand.

"Yes, Sadiq," said Mr. Kassim.

"My baba says it's to become better Muslims," said Sadiq. "Fasting helps us think about other people. They may not have food like we do."

"That's correct, Sadiq," Mr. Kassim said. "Fasting from sunrise to sunset teaches us what it might be like for others who struggle to get enough food."

"I am going to fast this year," said Zaza. "My hooyo said I could try it on the weekends."

"That's great, Zaza!" Mr. Kassim said, smiling. "Some of you may try to fast during Ramadan, like Zaza. Remember, it's important to talk to your parents about it first."

The kids nodded as they listened to Mr. Kassim.

"Okay, time to go home, children," Mr. Kassim said. "***Salaam!***"

“Salaam, Mr. Kassim!” Sadiq, Zaza, and Manny called out together.

* * *

That night, Sadiq talked to his parents about his idea for the iftar. The next day, he invited Zaza and Manny over after school. They all flopped on the floor of Sadiq’s room.

“I thought about what Mr. Kassim said yesterday,” said Sadiq. “What do you think about hosting an iftar? We could ask people to donate money for the meal. Then we could give the money to Al-Iqra.”

“I like that idea. Let’s make it a club. I bet we can find some others to join us,” Zaza said.

Manny jumped up. "The Money Makers Club!" he shouted.

"Good idea, Manny," said Sadiq, laughing.

"Okay. Where should we do it?" asked Zaza.

"I asked Hooyo if we could do it here," said Sadiq. "She doesn't think we will have enough space. She said we might be able to have it at the masjid."

"Cool!" said Manny.

"Hooyo spoke to the **imam** already," Sadiq said. "She asked if we could use it the first Saturday of Ramadan for our fundraiser. He said we could!"

"Great! What should we do about food?" asked Manny.

CONSTELLATIONS

"We will need help cooking," said Zaza. "Should we ask our parents?"

"Or we could ask people to bring a dish," said Manny. "That way everyone can share their food."

"That's a great idea!" said Sadiq. "Let's design a flyer. We can put that on there."

"You should do the artwork," said Manny. "I like your drawings in art class."

"You do?" asked Sadiq, smiling.

Manny nodded. "Can you draw a new moon and some stars around the border?"

"Yes, but only if you help me," said Sadiq. He took out his drawing kit from under the bed.

The boys worked on their flyer until they had a design they were proud of. Then it was time for Manny and Zaza to go home. They decided to meet the next day to continue planning.

I hope we can get some more friends to join our club by then! thought Sadiq. He planned to invite some friends tomorrow at school.

CHAPTER 2

PLANNING THE IFTAR

Tuesday after school, the boys were in Sadiq's room talking about their new club. Nuurali was sitting at the computer and writing.

"I talked to Yusuf and Ahlam at school," said Sadiq. "I told them about the Money Makers Club. They asked if they could join. I told them we would meet every day after school to plan."

Yusuf and Ahlam were twins. They were in Sadiq's class at school.

"Of course they can join," said Manny. "They can help with the iftar!"

"My hooyo says Ramadan is the busiest time of the year," said Zaza. "We should start inviting people to come soon."

"We should hang up flyers at school," said Manny.

"That's a great idea, Manny," said Sadiq. "But how will we get grown-ups to come too? They will be donating the most money."

"You should start a website or something," Nuurali suggested, looking up from the computer.

"That's a great idea, Nuurali!" said Sadiq.

“I could help you make one on Help-a-Cause,” Nuurali offered. “It’s a website for raising money. Just tell me what you need.”

“But how will people know about it?” asked Manny.

“I bet Baba can help,” said Nuurali. “He can ask the imam to email it out to everyone.”

"What do you think, Zaza?" asked Sadiq.

"Huh?" said Zaza. He had been staring out the window.

"Nuurali offered to help us," said Manny. "He can start a fundraising page online."

"Uh . . . yeah," said Zaza. "That's great. Thank you, Nuurali."

"We should record a video for the website asking people to donate money and come to the iftar," said Manny. "We can explain what the donations will be used for."

"Yes! I bet we could borrow Baba's phone!" said Sadiq.

"That should be pretty easy to do," said Nuurali.

"Do you have any ideas, Zaza?" asked Sadiq. He noticed his friend hadn't been talking much.

"Yeah, I like the website," replied Zaza. "I have a lot of homework tonight. I'm going to go home."

"Okay . . ." said Sadiq.

Zaza walked out of the room.

Why doesn't Zaza seem to want to be a part of this? Sadiq wondered. He turned toward Manny and Nuurali

"Is Zaza okay?" asked Nuurali. "He seemed distracted."

Sadiq shrugged. *I wonder if he'll come to our meeting tomorrow,* he thought.

* * *

The next day, Sadiq, Nuurali, Manny, Zaza, Ahlam, and Yusuf met in Sadiq's front yard. They were going to film their video. Zaza had shown up, but he did not seem happy to be there.

"Stand together in a line," said Nuurali. He held Baba's phone in his hand. "That way I can get all of you in the picture. What do you want people to know?"

"The location of the iftar," said Manny.

"And why we're raising money," said Ahlam.

"We should say the date and time of the event," said Yusuf.

"And we should ask people to bring a dish to share," added Sadiq. "Just like on the flyer."

Zaza stood quietly behind the rest of the group.

What's wrong with Zaza? Sadiq thought. *Why is he being so quiet?*

"What else do we need?" asked Manny. "Zaza?"

"Hmm?" replied Zaza.

"What else do we need in our video?" asked Sadiq. Zaza didn't seem interested at all. "You're not listening again, Zaza! Just like yesterday!"

"Whatever you guys said is fine," replied Zaza, looking at the ground and kicking the dirt.

"Is something wrong, Zaza?" asked Sadiq. "You usually have great ideas for our clubs."

Zaza shook his head but didn't say anything.

Sadiq was growing frustrated with his friend. *Why won't Zaza tell us what's going on?* he wondered.

"Nuurali, can we shoot the video tomorrow instead?" Sadiq asked.

"Sure," said Nuurali.

"Let's go print the flyers," said Manny. "We could walk around the neighborhood now and hang them up."

"Do you want to help with *that*?" Sadiq asked Zaza.

"Actually, I think I need to go home," said Zaza, staring at the ground. "I have to help my mom with something." He started to walk toward the sidewalk.

"Okay," said Sadiq. "Well, let us know if you have any ideas for the iftar. Bye, Zaza."

Zaza waved to the Money Makers Club and headed down the street. Sadiq wondered if they had just lost one of their members. He felt sad that Zaza wasn't there, but he was excited to keep planning the iftar.

Sadiq led the way back into the house. The boys gathered around the computer to look at their flyer.

Nuurali had helped them design it and scan it on the computer. He'd even added it to their Help-a-Cause page. They had also added the website to the flyer. The Money Makers Club was proud of the design they'd come up with.

"I'll print some copies of the flyers," said Nuurali. "You can grab them from Baba's printer in his room."

Sadiq went to get the flyers. He also grabbed a stapler from Baba's desk to hang the flyers on telephone poles and bulletin boards. He came back to his friends with a stack of flyers.

"Okay, let's go!" said Nuurali.

"Please be back in time for dinner!" Hooyo called.

AL-IQRA
SCHOOL
FUNDRAISER

"Okay," Nuurali and Sadiq said to their mother as they walked outside.

"How will we know who is going to come?" Manny asked once they were all outside. "We should come up with a plan so we know we'll have enough food."

"I added an RSVP option to the website," said Nuurali. "People can respond if they are coming and say what dish they will bring."

"Most people are donating online, right?" asked Ahlam.

Nuurali nodded.

"What if people bring money to donate?" asked Manny. "We'll need a way to collect it."

"The masjid has locked donation boxes. People can put the money in there," said Yusuf.

"Great!" said Manny.

"Salaam, Mr. Ibrahim!" Manny suddenly called out.

Mr. Ibrahim was their neighbor. He was walking toward them on the sidewalk.

"Salaam, boys!" said Mr. Ibrahim.

The boys gave him a flyer. "What is this?" Mr. Ibrahim asked.

"It's an invitation to our iftar," said Sadiq, beaming. "Would you like to come with your family?"

"I would love to!" said Mr. Ibrahim. "I see it's this Saturday."

"Yes," said Manny. "We are raising money to help a Dugsi in Somalia."

"That's great!" said Mr. Ibrahim. "I can't wait!"

The boys spent the afternoon walking around the neighborhood. They gave a flyer to everyone they met. Many neighbors promised to come.

When it started to get dark, the boys headed home. Sadiq ran all the way back, and Nuurali tried to keep up. Sadiq was excited to keep planning the iftar! But he still wondered why Zaza didn't want to participate.

CHAPTER 3

CLUB PROBLEMS

"Do you think we should look up recipes?" asked Manny. "What should we make for our dishes?"

"Maybe pilaf?" replied Sadiq. "Hooyo has a recipe that I like."

"And curry!" said Manny.

"Sambuus!" said Yusuf.

The Money Makers Club was at the library the next day. Sadiq had been surprised to see that Zaza showed up. Nuurali had also come to help.

"You're so quiet, Zaza," said Ahlam. "Do you have any ideas for food?"

Zaza shrugged.

"Let's go online to find recipes," said Sadiq. "We can print them out to take home and cook."

Everyone got up, but Zaza didn't move.

"I'll wait here with Zaza," said Ahlam, sitting back down.

Nuurali, Manny, and Yusuf walked away to the computer section. Sadiq decided to stay behind.

"Is something wrong, Zaza?" Sadiq asked. "You seem sad."

Zaza frowned. "I just want to do something else instead," he said.

"Instead of the iftar?" asked Ahlam.

"The iftar is great," said Zaza. "But I want to focus on a different cause for Ramadan this year. I want to collect blankets for babies in the hospital."

"Why?" asked Sadiq. He started to feel upset. "We already agreed to the iftar."

"Well I wanted to—" started Zaza.

"That's really unfair, Zaza!" said Sadiq. He didn't understand why his friend was backing out now. "You agreed to join the club."

"I know but—" said Zaza.

"Never mind," said Sadiq. He stood and walked to the computer station.

"I don't know why he's mad at me," Zaza said to Ahlam. "I just wanted to explain." He looked down at his hands.

"Don't be sad, Zaza," said Ahlam.

"But he's my best friend, and he won't listen," Zaza said.

"I'm sure Sadiq didn't mean it," Ahlam said. "Let's go see what recipes they found."

Zaza sat quietly as Ahlam walked away. After a moment, he stood up and left the library without saying anything to his friends.

* * *

Later that night, Sadiq sat at the kitchen table. His parents were cleaning up around the kitchen. Nuurali sat nearby doing homework.

"Are you ready to host the iftar, Sadiq?" asked Baba.

"I don't know, Baba," replied Sadiq.

"Why are you unsure?" asked Baba.

"Well, Zaza hasn't been helping," said Sadiq. "Every time we ask him what he thinks, he shrugs. I don't know what to do."

"Have you asked him what's wrong?" asked Hooyo.

"I did ask him," said Sadiq. "He wants to start his own fundraiser."

“What’s wrong with that, qalbi?” Baba asked.

“We already have a plan for the iftar,” said Sadiq. “He seemed excited about it at first. I don’t know why he doesn’t want to do it now.”

“Ahlam told me that Zaza did try to explain why,” Nuurali said kindly. “You didn’t let him finish.”

“The Money Makers Club already agreed to raise money for the Dugsi,” said Sadiq. “If there are two causes, there will be less money for the Dugsi.”

“I understand why you’re worried, Sadiq,” said Hooyo. “But it’s important we all care for one another. We can do this in different ways.”

Sadiq nodded.

"It doesn't *have* to be raising money for the school," Hooyo went on. "And in your case, the iftar could be raising money for both causes—yours and Zaza's."

"Yes, Hooyo," replied Sadiq.

"It sounds like Zaza was trying to help in his own way. But he should have told you how he was feeling," said Baba.

"Yes, Baba," said Sadiq. "I think I understand now. He tried to tell me what was going on, and I got upset. Tomorrow I'll talk to him and apologize."

"That's great!" said Baba, smiling. "You two will be friends again before you know it!"

CHAPTER 4

BACK TO NORMAL

Friday morning was bright and sunny. Sadiq stopped at Zaza's house on his way to the bus stop. Zaza's mother, Mrs. Feiza, opened the door when he knocked.

"Salaam, ***Habo*** Feiza!" said Sadiq.

"Salaam, Sadiq," replied Zaza's mom, smiling. "Are you here to see Zaza?"

"I am walking to the bus stop," said Sadiq. "Does Zaza want to walk with me?"

"He should be coming down any minute," replied Feiza.

A moment later, Zaza dashed down the stairs with his backpack.

"Salaam, Hooyo," said Zaza. He waved goodbye to his mom.

Sadiq looked down as they left. "Hi, Zaza," he said.

"Hi, Sadiq," said Zaza.

"I wanted to say I am sorry for not listening to you," said Sadiq. "What was your idea?"

"I tried to explain yesterday. But I should've told you sooner," said Zaza. "After our first meeting, I talked with my mom. I got an idea for a different cause."

"What is it?" asked Sadiq.

"My hooyo's sister is a doctor at the hospital," said Zaza. "She delivers babies. Habo Fahima said sometimes the babies' parents are poor. They can't afford things like blankets."

"Oh no!" said Sadiq.

"Habo says people knit blankets. Or they donate extra blankets they have at home," said Zaza. "When parents leave the hospital, they get a blanket. I wanted to ask people to donate baby blankets."

"I'm sorry, Zaza," Sadiq said. "I thought people would donate to one cause only. I thought there would be less for the Dugsi. But I talked with my parents. I realized I was wrong. We can help people in many ways."

"Thank you, Sadiq," said Zaza.

"Maybe we can find a way to help both causes?" Sadiq asked.

Zaza nodded and smiled. "I would like that."

* * *

That afternoon, Sadiq and Zaza told Manny, Yusuf, and Ahlam about their talk.

"We want to find a way to combine the two causes," Sadiq said. "We can put the donation boxes on one table. People can give money to either cause—or both if they want. And we'll set up another table for the blankets."

"That's a great idea, Sadiq!" said Manny.

"We can make a poster to explain what the baby blankets are for," said Zaza.

"Nuurali told me last night that he could also send out an email to everyone who has sent an RSVP," said Sadiq. "We can ask them to bring any extra blankets they have. We can also let them know that they can donate to the hospital as well as the Dugsi."

"Awesome!" said Yusuf.

"Did you guys ask your families if they will help?" asked Sadiq.

"Yes," replied Ahlam. "Our parents are coming to help us. We are bringing food as well."

"I'll be there with my parents," said Zaza. "My brothers are coming too!"

"My baba is coming with me," said Manny.

"Are we serving the food?" asked Ahlam.

Sadiq nodded. "I asked my parents to help with that," he said. "Nuurali and Aliya said they will serve as well."

"Our parents will bring drinks," said Yusuf. "Bottled water and juice."

"Zaza, are you in charge of plates?" asked Manny. "Could you also bring napkins?"

"Yes!" replied Zaza.

The kids got to work on their posters and decorations for the event.

As they talked and planned, Sadiq smiled. *The Money Makers Club is back to normal,* he thought. *The iftar tomorrow will be so much fun!*

CHAPTER 5

THE BIG EVENT

On Saturday afternoon, Sadiq and his mom made rice pilaf with goat meat. It was one of Sadiq's favorite meals! He sniffed the air and smelled garlic and ginger. He loved the spices in this dish.

When they were done cooking, Sadiq's family helped him pack the food and decorations into the car. Then they all got into their car and drove to the masjid.

When they arrived, Sadiq went to find his friends. Yusuf and Ahlam were setting up a table for blanket donations for the hospital.

"Hi, you guys!" called Sadiq. "You got here before us!"

"Just by a few minutes," said Yusuf.

"I hope people saw the email about the blankets," said Ahlam.

"Me too," said Sadiq. Then he went to find Manny and Zaza. "Hey, guys," he said when he spotted them. "Want to help me set up the donation tables?"

"Yes!" said Manny. He pointed to a table leaning against a wall nearby. "Here's a folding table. I think we just need to extend the legs."

As they set up the tables, food, and decorations, the boys were quiet. They wanted to raise a lot of money for both causes and collect a lot of blankets! They were nervous.

Soon there was a line forming at the door. Sadiq recognized many people who walked in. But there was one woman he had never seen before. Mr. Kassim was introducing her to people. Soon they walked over to the club.

"Here is the group that organized the iftar," said Mr. Kassim. "This is Sadiq, Zaza, Manny, Yusuf, and Ahlam. Kids, this is Mrs. Deeqa Hassan. She works for the charity that is helping Al-Iqra school."

BLANKETS

"We're the Money Makers!" said Zaza.

"Salaam, kids!" said Mrs. Hassan. "You've done a lovely job with the iftar!"

"Mr. Kassim told us about how this will help the children at Al-Iqra," said Sadiq.

"Yes," replied Mrs. Hassan. "It has been a tough year. This will mean the world to the Al-Iqra school. And donating blankets to a local hospital is also a wonderful idea."

"That was all Zaza!" said Sadiq, smiling.

Sadiq looked outside. The sun had gone down.

AL-IQRA SCHOOL
FUNDRAISER!!

Inside, people were finding places to sit. Everyone was getting ready to break their fast. Sadiq was proud of all the work his club had done.

"Thank you for all your hard work," said Mrs. Hassan. "I think I have to give a short speech now."

Mrs. Hassan walked to the front of the room. Everyone quieted down.

"Thank you for all your kindness," Mrs. Hassan said to the crowd. "I know the kids at Al-Iqra school in Somalia will be very happy!"

"We are very happy to help," said Baba from the back of the room. "All kids deserve a chance to learn!"

“I’m so glad we made a difference!” said Sadiq.

“Me too,” said Zaza. “And I’m glad we are donating baby blankets!”

“The Money Makers Club has helped two causes so far,” said Manny.

“And I’m sure we can find more to help!” said Sadiq. No matter what cause he and his friends would help next, he knew they’d be in it together.

GLOSSARY

afford (uh-FORD)—to have enough money to buy something

charity (CHAYR-uh-tee)—kindness; or a group that raises money or collects goods to help people in need

curry (KUR-ee)—a dish seasoned with a blend of spices called curry

design (di-ZYN)—to draw a plan for something that can be made

donation (doh-NAY-shuhn)—a gift

Dugsi (DHUG-see)—Islamic school

fast (FAST)—to give up eating for a period of time

fundraiser (FUHND-ray-zer)—an event held to raise money

introduce (in-truh-DOOS)—to cause to be known by name

invitation (in-vi-TAY-shuhn)—a written or spoken request for someone to go somewhere or do something

lunar calendar (LOO-nur KAL-uhn-dur)—a calendar that follows the cycles of the moon traveling around Earth

pilaf (pi-LAF)—a dish made of seasoned rice and meat

Ramadan (RAH-muh-dahn)—the ninth month of the Muslim year, when Muslims fast each day from sunrise to sunset

recognize (REK-uhg-nize)—to see someone and know who the person is

shrug (SHRUHG)—to raise your shoulders to show that you don't know or don't care about someone or something

sliver (SLIV-ur)—a very thin piece of something

TALK ABOUT IT

1. Zaza doesn't seem to want to help out with the Money Makers Club. What are some ways you could tell Zaza is upset?

2. Sadiq and his friends raise money and donate blankets for their charity. Discuss ideas of things you could do to help your own community.

3. Nuurali tries to film a video for the iftar, but it doesn't go well. Discuss what went wrong and how it could have gone better.

WRITE IT DOWN

1. Sadiq wants to help the Al-Irqa school in Somalia. Write a list of places you would like to help out if you were collecting donations.

2. Sadiq gets mad when Zaza says he wants to help out another cause. What could Sadiq have done differently? Write a scene where Sadiq reacts to Zaza in a different way.

3. What are the ways Sadiq plans to get donations for the Money Makers Club? Write down the ideas listed in the book.

Zaza wants to collect baby blankets to donate to the hospital. Create your own blanket for yourself or to donate!

WHAT YOU NEED:

- fleece fabric
- scissors
- ruler
- writing utensil
- construction paper

WHAT TO DO:

1. Pick what colors you'd like to use for your blanket. If you decide you want two different kinds of fabric, make sure you have enough for two sides of the blanket.

2. Using the scissors, carefully trim two pieces from your fabric.

3. Line up the two pieces so both have their fuzzy side facing out.

4. Trim the two pieces of fabric so they are the same size.

5. Using a ruler, measure and draw a square on the construction paper. Make sure it's a size that will fit on the corners of your blanket. Cut out the paper.

6. Place the square on each corner of the fabrics and use it as a guide to cut a square out of the fabric. Make sure to cut through both layers.

7. Once all four corners have squares cut out of them, cut a fringe on all the sides of the blanket, or a line every inch on the fabrics. Use the ruler to measure your cuts if needed.

8. Begin tying the fringes of the top piece of fabric to the fringes on the bottom piece. Go around the blanket until all the top fringes are tied to the bottom ones. Once they're all snugly tied, your blanket is complete!

CREATORS

Siman Nuurali grew up in Kenya. She now lives in Minnesota. Siman and her family are Somali—just like Sadiq and his family! She and her five children love to play badminton and board games together. Siman works at Children's Hospital, and in her free time, she also enjoys writing and reading.

Anjan Sarkar is a British illustrator based in Sheffield, England. Since he was little, Anjan has always loved drawing stuff. And now he gets to draw stuff all day for his job. Hooray! In addition to the Sadiq series, Anjan has been drawing mischievous kids, undercover aliens, and majestic tigers for other exciting children's book projects.